A Song for Acadia

A Song for Acadia

Mary Alice Downie and George Rawlyk
Illustrated by Ron Berg

NIMBUS
PUBLISHING

Nimbus Publishing Limited
PO Box 9166
Halifax, NS   B3K 5M8
(902) 455-4286

Printed and bound in Canada
Interior design: Terri Strickland

National Library of Canada Cataloguing in Publication

Downie, Mary Alice, 1934-
A song for Acadia / by Mary Alice Downie and George
Rawlyk ; illustrated by Ron Berg.

Originally published: Toronto : Kids Can Press, 1980, under title: A proper
Acadian.

ISBN 1-55109-474-6
1. Acadians–Expulsion, 1755–Juvenile fiction. I. Rawlyk, George A., 1935-1995.
II. Berg, Ron III. Title.

PS8557.O85P76 2004   C813'.54   C2004-901378-5

Canadä   The Canada Council | Le Conseil des Arts
          for the Arts | du Canada

We acknowledge the financial support of the Government of Canada
through the Book Publishing Industry Development Program (BPIDP)
and the Canada Council for our publishing activities.

To Anna and Miriam,
Christine, Jocelyn and Alexandra

Author's note

A *Song for Acadia* is based, in part, on a manuscript by Church of Scotland minister Andrew Brown (1763–1834), who was sent to St. Matthew's Church in Halifax in 1787. Fascinated by the history of North America, Dr. Brown collected and copied original documents, corresponded with scholars, and interviewed officials and elderly Acadians who had managed to make their way home after the Deportation. After his death, Dr. Brown's papers—among them drafts of his unfinished history of Nova Scotia—were scattered. Some were donated to the British Museum in 1852, some ended up in the archives at Edinburgh University. Much of this material is accessible through The Public Archives of Canada and Nova Scotia Archives and Records Management.

Boston 1754

THE MOON BROKE through the clouds and Timothy edged further into the shadow of the warehouse wall. He looked quickly along the stretch of high fence. The road was empty.

"Fool," he muttered to himself. He knew that he shouldn't have come. All he wanted now was to get it over with. He swore he would never do *this* again.

He shivered in the darkness, waiting for the next break in the clouds. When it came, moonlight flowed down the wet road silhouetting three watchmen with sticks, climbing the fence. Timothy managed two sharp whistles to warn the gang at the dock. The darkness came alive. Two men jumped over the fence to chase the thieves, the third ran towards him.

Timothy fled, but in his panic he turned into a blind alley. He clawed at the brick wall in front of him but he couldn't reach the top. Then a great hand caught the collar of his coat and shook him like a rat.

"Now, you thieving little rogue, let's see what you look like." The man dragged Timothy out of the alley into the moonlit street and jerked his head back to see his face.

"I know you," he said. "You're Samuel Parsons' youngest. What are you doing mixed up with these skulking wretches?" He loosened his grip on Timothy's collar to let him speak.

"Don't know, sir." Timothy hung his head and mumbled.

"Speak up, boy. I'm not going to bite you."

"It was a dare and I was stupid enough to do it."

"First time you did this?" asked the watchman. "Don't lie to me 'cause I'll know it."

"First time," said Timothy.

"I'll believe you for your father's sake. He's got enough problems just now being sick and out-of-work. He don't need trouble from you. Get off home as fast as you can. I'll be having a word with him in the morning."

Timothy bolted through the cobbled streets as if ten devils were after him. "Never again," he vowed as he ran.

TIMOTHY WAS HELPING his father to his chair in the front room of the cellar where they lived, when the watchman arrived next morning. He went quickly to open the door.

"Come in, Nathaniel," his father called. "I can't get up to welcome you. My leg is bothersome again."

"Sorry to see you like this, Samuel," said the watchman. "Has the boy told you why I'm here?"

"He has. And he knows how lucky he is that it was you and not somebody else who caught him."

"You stay away from that crew, young lad, they're up to no good," cautioned the watchman. He settled himself on the chair that Timothy brought him and pulled out his clay pipe.

"We've sorted things out now, Nathaniel," Samuel Parsons said. "Boston's no place for a boy with a sick father and no mother. I'm going to stay with my daughter Priscilla until the leg gets better and Tim's going to Acadia to live with his mother's sister for awhile. Priscilla's husband will take him up there. He sails tomorrow, which doesn't leave time for any more mischief."

"That's good news," said Nathaniel. "Why don't you sit down, lad. I'm not going to arrest you."

Timothy blushed and glanced at his father.

"Tim will stand for a bit, Nathaniel. The crime had its punishment before you arrived."

Both men looked at Timothy and then they all laughed— Timothy with relief that the sorry adventure was over.

"I hate to leave Boston and father," he said. "And I don't know if I'll like Acadia, but think of sailing with Ebenezer! That's something I've dreamed about. May I go now? I want to say goodbye to my friends."

He saw the watchman's stern glance. "Not those friends, sir. Even if I were staying in Boston, I'd keep away from them."

His father nodded. "Be back by midday. Your sister will be here to make the arrangements."

Timothy left and made his way slowly through the crooked streets of the city. He stopped at the blacksmith's to watch the forge glowing in the darkness and to listen to the hammers beating the red-hot iron. Shadowy figures moved back and forth, bent before the leaping flames. It was like the Reverend Mr. Sewell's fiery descriptions of hell. He stepped inside and a blast of heat smacked his face.

One of the workers came over. It was Rob, the smith's son. He was three years older than Timothy and, at fifteen, already as strong as a young giant.

"Well, Tim," he said, his face all streaky with soot and sweat, "ready to take a turn at the bellows?"

"Not today. I'm leaving for Acadia in the morning. I just wanted to say goodbye."

"Acadia!" Rob asked. "That's Nova Scotia, isn't it? Your mother's country. Well, good luck and watch out for bears.

They say the woods up there are full of them." He shook Timothy's hand and gave him a friendly slap on the back.

When Timothy got back out on the street, he rubbed his tingling shoulder. "If the bears are as big as Rob, I'd better be careful," he muttered.

"Don't talk to yourself or they'll lock you up." The teasing voice from behind startled him.

Timothy turned around. "Well, it's Abigail Sewell," he said. "Who let you out of church so early in the morning?"

Abigail smoothed her long curls. "A little more time in church might do you good," she said calmly. "I saw you sneaking out early last Sunday. That's when you said nasty things about my father."

"Me, say nasty things about the Reverend Mr. Sewell? Not me."

"Oh, don't put on that butter-wouldn't-melt-in-my-mouth expression with me," Abigail said. "You told Rob that Father looked and sounded like a mad turkey on Thanksgiving when he preached."

"Must have been someone else," Timothy said. "I like turkeys. But wait, today we'll declare a truce. I leave for Acadia tomorrow and I don't want to go with a bad conscience."

"Acadia! Then you'll have to speak French. Do you know how?"

"I'd forgotten about that," Timothy said. "I haven't really spoken any since my mother died five years ago. I hope I can remember some of it."

"Your mother was French, wasn't she?"

"She was Acadian and that's different. They came from France long ago but to call them French would be like calling you English."

"Do they fight for France?" she persisted.

"I don't think so, but even if they do, I won't," he promised.

"I think you'd fight anybody, just for the fun of it."

"We have a truce, remember? Let's go up Fort Hill and count ships."

When they reached the top of the hill, Timothy and Abigail sat on the grass and looked down over the bay. Schooners, sloops and men-of-war lay anchored in the harbour, while dozens of sails scudded across the choppy blue water. Seagulls squawked and fought over the refuse that had been tossed overboard. Ships, bound for England, the West Indies and Acadia, were being loaded and unloaded all along the busy wharves.

Timothy recognized the dock where he had kept watch last night. He shivered and turned to Abigail, who was making herself a large dandelion wreath.

"Come on, Abby, I have to go now. I promised to be home by midday to see my sister."

"Father's sermons will seem even longer without you to make faces at," she said. She put the wreath on her head and followed him slowly down the hill.

When Timothy reached home, dinner was ready. "Just in time, for a change," Priscilla said approvingly. "I was telling Father that I'm glad he's decided to be sensible. The two of you living alone here when he needs someone to look after him was...."

Priscilla tended to leave sentences unfinished as she bustled about her work. Timothy felt sorry for his father. Priscilla would look after him well enough, but her exacting ways would be hard to endure.

"Just look at the way you two live," she exclaimed.

"Everything is a mess. Do you ever comb your hair, Timothy? It makes you look like a hedgehog the way it sticks up at the back. Where are your clothes, Timothy? They must be washed and mended. Look at this...."

She disappeared into the tiny back bedroom in search of laundry. Timothy and his father ate in silence. "Don't worry, lad," said his father. "This persecution will just help me get well sooner."

Timothy spent the afternoon working under the eagle eye of his sister. He scrubbed shirts and darned socks until his fingers ached and bled. By the time she was ready to leave, he had packed his few belongings in an old bag of his father's. Neatly, of course. The cellar windows sparkled and he felt that he could have eaten from the floor. Even the wood was stacked in tidy piles instead of a tumbled heap by the fireplace.

"There now!" Priscilla surveyed the scene of battle like a proud general. "Always leave a place better than you found it. I'll be here with the carriage for you tomorrow, Father." She paused and Timothy caught a glimpse of the sister he had known when he was very young, before she had married and become a respectable matron.

"Don't worry about Father," she said quietly. "I really will look after him. Take care of yourself away up there. I'll miss you and all your wicked ways." She smiled, kissed him and was gone.

Samuel Parsons talked late into the night with his son about Acadia and happier times long ago, when he had his own small fishing boat and had sailed along the Nova Scotia coast. There he had met and married Timothy's mother and had brought her back to Boston.

"You'll sail again, Father," Timothy said. "And then I'll go with you."

"I believe you, lad. I hope and pray that our luck has started to take a turn for the better. But you must get some sleep if you're to be up early in the morning. Ebenezer will want to be off with the first tide."

It was still dark when his father called. Timothy splashed cold water on his face and dressed quickly. He took a piece of bread and cheese to eat on the way and slung his bag over his shoulder.

"Goodbye, Father." He didn't say more. He was afraid he might cry which would embarrass them both.

"God be with you, my son." Samuel Parsons rose, with difficulty, to his feet.

"Sit down, Father. Your leg will hurt."

"I can still see my youngest to the door, even if I can't manage to the dock," his father said with determination.

They shook hands and with a last wave Timothy turned the corner and headed for the harbour. As he walked through the dark sleeping streets he came to the chestnut tree beside the Sewells' house. A single light from a window shone through the rustling branches. That would be the Reverend Mr. Sewell. Abigail had told him that her father often rose early to pray and study. Timothy could picture him writing furiously at his desk, with his floppy red wig hanging crooked over one eye.

"I won't miss those two-hour sermons," he thought, and he began to run towards the harbour.

THE RELIANT ROCKED gently beside the Long Wharf, ready to sail with the tide. The crew was busy stowing the last of the cargo.

"You're in good time, lad," called a voice from the bow. Timothy looked up and saw Ebenezer, in the pale predawn light, leaning against the rail and smoking his pipe. He was a small man, soberly dressed, with a deep voice and a quiet manner.

Timothy climbed aboard and went up to the bow, past coils of ropes on the deck.

"What are you trading on this trip?" he asked, once he'd reached Ebenezer's side.

"Axes, saws, pots, blankets, some good furniture and fine red cloth."

"Why red cloth?" Timothy asked.

"You'll see when we get to Minas. Now stow your gear and make yourself comfortable. We sail in half an hour. I'm glad to have you aboard."

Although Timothy had visited *The Reliant* several times and knew most of the crew, he had never been on a voyage before. Ebenezer made several trips a year to Nova Scotia, trading with the English at Halifax and Annapolis Royal, which was legal, and with the French at the fog-shrouded grey fortress of Louisbourg, which was not. Most of the New England merchants did this and no one thought worse of them for it.

Soon the crew cast off and the work of hoisting sail began. From his perch high in the rigging, Timothy saw the town grow smaller. The rising sun lit the church steeples and then Boston disappeared in a haze.

The winds were favourable and they made good progress. Timothy helped the cook after each meal and did odd jobs around the ship. He investigated every corner of *The Reliant*—from Ebenezer's comfortable cabin to the darkest, most spider-webbed corners of the hold that smelled of salt water, molasses and stale fish. At the end of each day, Ebenezer taught him French and told stories about Acadia.

"Your Uncle Pascal Poirier is one of the Elders of the village," Ebenezer said. "He's a good farmer and a kind man. And if you are thinking of a stern New England farmer when I say that, you are due for a pleasant surprise. The Acadians are a merry-hearted people. You'll hear more laughter in a day in Acadia than in a month in Boston."

He chuckled to himself and Timothy thought about the gradual change he'd noticed in his sober brother-in-law during the time they'd been at sea. The dark clothes of the Boston merchant had been put into a chest and he had become Ebenezer the sea captain. Each day he became livelier, whistling as he walked the decks. Timothy remembered the stories he'd heard in Boston that Ebenezer Trumble had been a privateer in his youth. He hadn't believed them, but now he wondered.

"Only three days and we're in the Bay of Fundy already," Ebenezer said. "With luck we'll be in Minas tomorrow."

"Does Aunt Madeleine know that I'm coming?"

"She does and she doesn't. We've talked about you many times over the past few years. She often said that she'd like to have you stay with them. Your mother and your Aunt Madeleine were very close and she'll love you as one of her own."

"I don't know much about my mother," Timothy said. "I remember her stories and I can still sing a few of her songs, but it's hard to recall what she looked like."

"It will all come back when you see your aunt. She and your mother were as like as two peas in a pod."

Ebenezer beckoned to one of the crew. "William, bring your flute here. You know tunes from all along the coast," he said. "Play an Acadian song, and let's see if Timothy remembers the words."

William began to play softly. Nothing happened at first but then Timothy found words stirring, coming from somewhere deep in his memory. He began to sing.

When he finished there was a moment's quiet and then everyone applauded.

"Timothy, my lad, you are full of surprises," Ebenezer boomed. "I didn't know you had such a fine voice. Another song, William."

Timothy sang again—a sea shanty this time—and everyone joined in the chorus. The ship cut smoothly through the dark water.

They sailed closer to shore the next day, past red cliffs and forests that came down to the water's edge. Now there were clearings with small houses and sometimes a church spire soaring against the green background of the hills. Horned cattle grazed in the wide meadows.

"There it is, Timothy," Ebenezer shouted. "There's Minas."

Timothy saw a small village perched on a slight upland between the forest and the shore. There were no streets, only a grassy pathway edged with a long straggling row of small loghouses with thatched or birchbark roofs. Large barns and outbuildings sat behind the houses.

The Reliant was secured to a mooring buoy and Timothy prepared to go ashore. Ebenezer picked out a bolt of red cloth, an axe and a saw and put them into the rowboat. Timothy climbed down after him with his bag.

The crew was already busy unloading the cargo. In exchange for these goods the Acadians would give Ebenezer chickens and pigs, peas and codfish, eels and hay. He would take all kinds of furs back to Boston, too, and feathers for beds.

Timothy and Ebenezer rowed ashore.

Although it was early, Minas was already bustling with people. "It's not much like Boston," Timothy said, staring at a group of old women who were clustered around a well. The air was filled with their laughter.

"Stop gawking," Ebenezer said. "You'll have time to see everything twice over."

"But look!" Timothy exclaimed, "All the old people are dressed in dark grey clothes and all the young ones are wearing green."

"That's because they dye their own cloth and those are the only two colours they have. Now you can see why my red cloth is popular. It fetches a handsome price here."

As they walked farther along the path, they passed a tall, gaunt man in a black cloak with a big silver cross hanging from his neck. He stared at Timothy with the keen eyes of a hawk.

"Who's that?" Timothy asked with a shiver.

"Father Felix Leneuf, the priest. You'll see him often. The Acadians go to church almost every day for one reason or another. There's always a wedding or a festival or a service. They love their land, their families and the church and haven't much use for anything else—which may bring trouble upon them some day." Ebenezer hesitated as if he wanted to say more. They came to a cabin that was larger than the rest and he stopped.

"We're here." He knocked on the door and a woman opened it. She had been baking and wiped floury fingers on her apron.

"Ebenezer!" she cried joyfully and threw her arms around him.

"I have a present for you," he said. He gave her the bolt of red cloth. "And a surprise," he added, as he stepped aside. Timothy had been standing right behind him.

"Timothy!" she cried. "I'd know him anywhere, Ebenezer." She hugged them both and called into the house, "Martin, come quickly. Your cousin's here."

All this was in French. Although Timothy didn't understand everything that was said, he knew he'd had a warm welcome.

"Come in, come in." Aunt Madeleine was both smiling and crying. "You remind me so much of your mother. Here's Martin now."

Timothy looked and looked again. Now he understood why his aunt had recognized him so easily. Behind her stood a tall skinny boy about his own age. A shock of hair stood straight up on the back of his head. If the hair had been brown instead of black, Timothy could have been looking in a mirror.

Martin grinned and began to talk rapidly. Despite his French lessons with Ebenezer, Timothy understood very little.

Aunt Madeleine noticed his confusion. "Set his bag over here beside the bed, Martin, then you can show him around the village," she said, speaking slowly. "He'll need to get his land legs back after the journey. Ebenezer, will you have a glass of cider?"

The boys were shy with each other at first, but by the time they'd visited the barnyard, beehives, dovecot and the orchard, they had become friends.

They went down to the shore to see what was hiding in the pools left by the tide. They clambered up the hillside and even poked their heads into the church, which was big and dark and full of statues and incense. It was not at all like the simple white meetinghouse in Boston where the Reverend Mr. Sewell thundered about sin and salvation. It will be strange coming to church here, Timothy thought. The Acadians were Roman Catholics not Protestants like Timothy, but his father had told him that he should go to church with his relatives.

That evening, gathered around a table beside the enormous fireplace, the family ate a supper of bread and milk and cheese. The grownups sat on plain wooden chairs; Timothy and Martin shared a chest covered with a huge, shaggy moosehide. They were to share one of the three big feather beds ranged against the walls of the house, too.

Ebenezer left early the next morning. After he'd gone, Timothy looked around the cabin. Martin had already gone with Uncle Pascal to do the chores. Aunt Madeleine was doing three things at once: sweeping the floor, clearing the breakfast dishes— they'd had pancakes mixed with slices of dried pork—and talking to the dog who lay drowsily by the fire nursing her puppies.

When Timothy went over to see them, one of the puppies nipped his finger. It was a fat little thing with floppy ears and a fluffy tail.

"That hurt," Timothy protested. The puppy nipped hungrily again. Timothy sucked his sore finger and stared into the fire. He was in Acadia at last but what was he to do now? He almost wished he could be back on *The Reliant* with Ebenezer. At least he'd had something to do there. Aunt Madeleine glanced at him, put away her broom and picked up her shawl.

"Dark thoughts, Timothy?" she said. "Come outside, let's look at the orchard." She led him along the pathway up to the grove behind the house.

The apple trees were planted in close rows, protected from the frosts of spring and the winds of autumn by a wide belt of willows. In the shade of a little arbour, wreathed in wild flowers, Aunt Madeleine sat him down and began to talk slowly in French with halting bits of English. She talked to Timothy of his mother, of the days long ago when his parents had met, of Acadia and its ways, of Martin and how they would be friends.

Aunt Madeleine reminded Timothy of his mother. She had the same flyaway brown hair and freckled face, the same brisk walk, and the same bursts of delighted laughter over such small things as an early mayflower or a brown egg still warm from the nest of a roving hen. She had the same quick anger too, he was to discover, like a flash of summer lightning.

Timothy enjoyed that morning in Acadia: the drowsy duet of bees humming and doves cooing, the faraway cries of sea birds and the sharp complaint of a goat. Apple blossoms drifted down to carpet the grass; willows shivered in the soft wind.

The church bell tolled, its deep tones ringing through the peaceful sounds of the valley. Aunt Madeleine brushed the pink blossoms from her hair and skirt and returned to the house. Timothy followed.

"This will be a good summer after all," he thought. "I'll have a lot to tell Father when I go back to Boston."

But it was not quite as easygoing as he expected. There was always work to be done even though the pigs fended for themselves in the woods and the cattle grazed contentedly on the salty hay of the marshes.

Aunt Madeleine was always busy cooking and washing and bread-making or looking after her large flock of chickens, ducks and partridges. Betweentimes she knitted and sewed with cloth that she made herself. Martin's three brothers and seven sisters often came to visit bringing their own families. Then, Aunt Madeleine would fill the pewter tankards with milk or cider and settle down for a good talk.

Timothy helped Martin with his chores and learned that farming was hard work. It was all so strange to him that at first he made many mistakes. When he tried to help repair the thatching on the barn, he fell through the roof. Luckily, he landed on a pile of hay and only his pride was hurt. Martin and Uncle Pascal laughed at his clumsy efforts, but always in a good-natured way. Gradually Timothy learned to laugh at himself.

One day as he was trying to milk the goat, she grew angry and lowered her horns menacingly. Timothy ran for the wall where Martin sat watching. The goat caught up with him just as he jumped. She butted him so hard that he flew over the wall and landed face down in a big mud puddle that the pigs had made. He skidded across the puddle for six feet before he stopped, with a bump, against the trough. He stood up, dripping mud from head to foot.

Martin wanted to laugh, but didn't dare. Timothy walked stiffly to the well where he poured water over his head until he

could see again. Then he walked back to the wall, climbed over, and proceeded to milk the goat in a workmanlike way. When he had finished, he handed the pail to Martin.

"Treat that with care. It wasn't easy to get."

Just then Aunt Madeleine came into the barnyard. "What are you two laughing about now?" she asked. Martin explained that Timothy had just won a battle with the goat.

"I hope you won't be too bruised to work tomorrow," she said. "Pascal needs you both to help with the new dyke."

"I'll be ready," Timothy assured her. He'd been looking forward to this.

"No need to wash your clothes," Martin said. "You'll just get them covered with mud again. Poor old Boston." Martin laughed so hard that he fell off the wall and landed in the mud himself.

UNCLE PASCAL AND his three older sons—René, Daniel and Mathieu—had already been working for days building the foundation of the dyke that ran across the marsh between two spits of higher ground. The base was almost twelve feet thick and was made of mud and large sods cut from the marsh. The dyke was to be five feet high and about two feet wide at the top. They had piled pieces of sod on top and, working from the high ground at each end of the dyke, they left a gap in the middle for the marsh water to flow out to sea.

It was Martin and Timothy's job to pack all the empty spaces tightly with soft clay so that no salty seawater could get through. The dyke had to be strong enough to hold out the sea at high tide.

Meanwhile, Uncle Pascal made the sluice that filled the gap in the centre. At low tide the gate opened to let the marsh water out. As the tide came in, it pushed the gate shut, keeping the sea water out.

"In a few years, this will be a fine field where we can grow hay and grain," Uncle Pascal told Timothy. They stood behind the completed dyke watching the sluice close and the tide build against the wall of clay. "We call the dyke *aboiteau*. Now that you've help build one, you're a proper Acadian."

Timothy felt very proud. He had enjoyed his part of the dyke-building. After that, whenever there was a dyke to be built or repaired, he was there. "Do be careful, Boston," Martin warned. "Don't stand too close to the dyke. You're so muddy all the time that we might get confused and build you into the wall."

By now Timothy felt completely at home in Minas. He spoke French so well that he could even follow most of the jokes and puns of which the Acadians were so fond.

His constant companion throughout the summer was the puppy that had bitten his finger when he first arrived in Minas. Aunt Madeleine gave her to Timothy when the puppy was old enough to leave her mother. He called her Nip and she followed him everywhere—except to the shore. Nip was afraid of the water and would stand back whining pitifully when Timothy and Martin were digging for clams or building the great fort of Louisbourg in the sand.

Much to his surprise, Timothy enjoyed the many church services he attended, although he still wasn't too fond of Father Leneuf. He loved singing the traditional responses, which were different from the gloomy hymns that were popular in Boston. As sung by the Acadians, these songs were an outpouring of joyful praise, and Timothy sang with all his heart. Even the priest would smile and encourage him, although he looked unfriendly when they met in the street.

"Why is he cross when he sees me?" Timothy asked at dinner one day, halting a large spoonful of rice, beans and beef that was on its way to his mouth. His appetite had certainly increased since he had come to Acadia.

"Father Leneuf is from France," Uncle Pascal answered. "The priests in Acadia don't like the English."

"But I'm from New England. I'm a Yankee."

"They don't like them, either."

"But why do the Acadians trade with us and seem friendly!"

"We've had to learn to live with the English because Acadia, or Nova Scotia as the English call our land, has belonged to England since 1713. All we ask is to be left alone and to be allowed to keep our religion, our language and our way of life. Long ago we had to swear an oath of allegiance to the English king, but we will never agree to bear arms against our French and Indian brothers. The English know this and have not forced us to make that promise."

Timothy was surprised by such a long speech. Aunt Madeleine and Martin talked so much that Uncle Pascal seldom had a chance to say more than "pass the bread." Timothy admired the gentle quiet man with his long white hair and kindly face.

"Father Leneuf told me that the new governor in Halifax wants us to swear the oath of allegiance again," Martin interrupted. "This time promising to bear arms."

"That, we can never do," Uncle Pascal declared firmly. Timothy had never seen him so agitated. "We are loyal to King George, but we do not want to take up arms against anyone. We bother no one and no one bothers us. We ask, 'Why should we fight when we have no enemies?' It is the kings and their soldiers who like to fight. Let them battle, let them die. Or they could live like us in peace.

"Besides, our friends the Mi'kmaq hate the English. If we took the oath they would think that we had betrayed them. They would attack our villages and burn our houses as they did at Beaubassin. Well, no more of our troubles. We Acadians have been caught between England and France for forty years and no great harm has come to us yet."

Silence greeted the end of his impassioned speech. Everyone listened when Uncle Pascal spoke, for they had great respect for his wisdom. He saw their concern and turned to Timothy. "No more dreary thoughts. Ebenezer will soon be coming for you, so we must enjoy your last few weeks in Acadia."

O NE DAY IN early August, after the boys had been picking
blueberries in the marsh, they found Ebenezer waiting at
the house.

"How's Father?" Timothy cried. "When do we leave? You'll
stay a few days this time, won't you? I have so much to tell
you."

Ebenezer and Aunt Madeleine exchanged worried glances.
"Your father is improving slowly," he said. "But the doctor
wishes us to care for him over the winter. You seem to be
thriving here and your Aunt Madeleine refuses to be parted
from you until next spring. Would you mind very much,
Timothy?"

"He *is* getting better?" Timothy asked. If he could just be
sure of that, he would be quite happy at the prospect of a few
more months in Minas. He did want to see the Harvest Festival.

"Yes, yes," Ebenezer reassured him. Timothy was so anxious
to show him Nip and the creek where he and Martin had built a
dam that he put Boston out of his mind.

The next morning he waved quite cheerfully as *The Reliant*
slipped away with the tide. "Give my love to Father and
Priscilla," he shouted. "Tell them that they should leave the
hurly-burly of Boston and come to Acadia for some peace and
quiet."

The fall was a busy time. There were crops to be harvested, wood to be gathered and briny hay to be collected from the undyked marshes for the cattle.

There was a roomy cellar beneath the house, its stone walls bound together with long moss. Aunt Madeleine stored her vegetables there in big Indian baskets: carrots, beets, onions, all sorts of greens, and squashes, multi-shaped and coloured. Only the cabbages were left in the field, pulled, to be covered and preserved by the snow. Timothy was pleased to see that there had been a fine crop, because Aunt Madeleine made a special turnip-cabbage-pork soup that he would willingly have eaten every day. Then there was the fruit: apples, of course, baskets and baskets of apples and pears and dried plums.

When all was ready for winter, it was time to celebrate the Harvest Festival. The whole village gathered in the churchyard to give thanks for the bounty of the land. The ceremony reminded Timothy of Thanksgiving in Boston.

The church sat by itself at the edge of a small bay. Its smooth lawn, made velvet by careful scything and rolling, was protected by a row of hemlocks and red flowering maples. The dead of Minas were buried here, beneath tall white crosses entwined with flowers. Timothy liked to sit in the graveyard occasionally, watching the sunset. It wasn't a gloomy spot at all.

The priest's house stood nearby, surrounded by a large garden.

"It holds all the medicinal plants used in the old herbals of Europe," Aunt Madeleine had told him. "And those of the Mi'kmaw wisemen too. Whenever we are sick, we go there to gather our medicine."

"Perhaps I'll be a priest and live here after Father Leneuf goes back to France," Timothy thought. "No, who ever heard of a Puritan priest? Priscilla wouldn't like it one bit."

Two months passed quickly and happily. Timothy was startled to realize that Christmas had come and gone, and it was already the first day of the New Year, the next important celebration in Acadia. He went with Uncle Pascal, Martin and the other men and boys from house to house in the village. They embraced everyone to renew old friendships and to ask forgiveness for bad things done and said. Then, before the service at the church, every family gathered at its own burying-place to remember the relatives they had lost.

Timothy thought of his mother. "She'd be glad that I like Acadia." He tried to repent for the bad things he had done during the last year. There was the dare in Boston, of course, when he'd nearly become part of a gang of dock thieves. To his surprise, he realized that was all he could think of. He'd been so busy learning that he'd had no time for any real mischief.

The rest of the winter passed quietly. The village looked entirely different with mounds of snow heaped beside the pathway and on the rooftops. Huge chunks of brown-coloured ice covered the flats and riverbanks and floated up and down with the changing of the tide.

Martin and Timothy often went snowshoeing in the woods. They loved to race in the sharp, clear winter air. They also helped Uncle Pascal cut timber for fuel and fencing. He repaired his tools for the spring and made new furniture for the cabin. He taught Timothy and Martin how to make chairs of their own.

There were parties most nights. Everyone crowded together into one house or another, no matter how small, to sing and talk. The younger people dressed up and performed plays, which Timothy was certain would never have been permitted in Boston. He was often asked to sing. The Acadians particularly liked the sea shanties he'd learned from Ebenezer. They didn't care much, however, for Priscilla's hymns.

Nip came to all the parties, too. No one minded because the Acadians were very fond of their animals. She had grown into a handsome little dog, afraid of nothing except water. She slept at Timothy's feet every night, buried in the warm mounds of the feather bed.

One April night Timothy and Martin, tired of the stuffiness and noise of the house, went for a walk. It had been raining and the paths were slippery with wet grass and mud. Martin sniffed the air.

"Spring, 1755," he said. "Soon you'll have been here for a whole year."

"Ebenezer will be coming any day. I'll be sorry to leave."

"I hope he doesn't come before the Festival of the Geese. That's the best celebration of all. Wait!" Martin stopped in the pathway and held up his hand for silence. "Listen."

At first Timothy could hear nothing except the familiar sounds of the night. Then he heard it, a faint chorus in the sky. The boys waited, wordless, among the dripping trees. The honking came closer. High above in the dark sky, a great V cut the moon in pieces. The first geese had returned.

Then there were busy times indeed as the crops were sown in the dyked marshland meadows. Timothy and Martin were up

many nights helping Uncle Pascal with the births of calves and lambs. They spent hours watching the baby ducklings swimming confidently in the brimming creek, unaware of the danger from foxes and gulls.

At last the Festival of the Geese arrived. It was time to celebrate the joy of being delivered from the cold and storms of winter. Again, the Acadians gathered in the churchyard. First there were prayers.

"Keep us from the plague of the caterpillar," Father Leneuf intoned. "Keep us from the plague of the grasshopper, the field mouse and other vermin. Keep in check the evil spirit of the birds that plague us." He turned his fierce eyes to his parishioners. "Remember Him in whose hand are all the armies that have life. He alone can commission the weakest of them to blight the beauty of the spring. For the glory of summer they can send a desolation yet more terrible than that of winter."

Then everyone joined in singing the responses. After that came the wandering through the fields. They walked two by two. First came the girls, dressed in white, with veils and wreaths of wild flowers. The old women followed, then the boys and the men. The Elders of the parish, Uncle Pascal among them were at the rear with the priest and his lay assistants.

The procession ended and the people scattered to their houses or stood in small groups chatting in the sunlight.

"Now for the feast," Martin said. "Someone is to be named tonight."

Timothy knew that the Acadians often gave each other nicknames. Martin was called Quill because of his hair. Aunt Madeleine was affectionately named the Musket because of her constant small explosions of anger. Only Uncle Pascal was spared because of the great respect the people in the village felt for him.

Timothy was frequently called Boston. He'd liked it at first but now he wished that he could be called something else. It seemed to set him apart from the others. But he knew that only some special act or change of character could alter a nickname once given.

The boys returned to the house where they found Aunt Madeleine and her daughters and daughters-in-law hard at work preparing for the feast. Wooden trenchers, pewter dishes and horn spoons had been set out on the table along with the barrels of cider, good French wine, and brandy smuggled in from Louisbourg. All day the women cooked and baked until there was not an inch of space left on the table.

"I have never been to such a grand feast!" said Timothy. After many hours of songs, jokes and riddles, Uncle Pascal slowly rose to his feet.

"It is time," he said with his usual dignity, "to bestow a new name upon our cousin from Boston. He has been with us for many months and must, alas, soon leave. We wish he could stay forever, for his singing has added much to our pleasures and we know that our dykes will never break with his firm hand repairing them. Let us give a toast now to Timothy who shall henceforth be known, not as Boston, but as Boiteau."

"Boiteau! That's a name I can be proud of. Nothing could be more Acadian than that!" Timothy thought. His face flushed with pride. "Thank you," he said, and prepared to make a speech as was the custom. But no more words came. "Thank you," he stammered and he sat down.

"A song," Martin called.

And so Timothy sang. He sang of the calm skies of the Bay of Fundy, of the boats of the fishermen returning with their catch, of the stillness of night descending, of the cheerful talk around the fire when day was done; he sang the songs of Acadia.

He was down at the shore several days later, still humming tunes from the feast, when he looked up and saw *The Reliant* sailing into the bay.

"Ebenezer," he cried and raced to the water to greet his brother-in-law when he came ashore.

"I've so much to tell you. I've helped deliver a lamb and I can repair dykes and milk a goat and they call me Boiteau. How is Father?"

"He's much better, although the doctor wants Priscilla to look after him still. He misses you and will be glad to see you again."

Suddenly Timothy realized that he didn't want to go. Not now, not with summer at hand and so many things yet to do. Uncle Pascal had promised to take them out into the bay to hunt the white porpoises from which they got their oil.

He looked disconsolately at his sandy feet. He'd almost forgotten the feeling of shoes. He'd be a fine sight in his sister's big old house on Brattle Street with its heavy curtains and silver candlesticks and Turkish carpets.

"Can't I come in the fall? Father will be truly well then and I can look after him at home."

"I'd like to take you now, Timothy. Great troubles are coming upon the Acadians. Britain and France are at war." Timothy had never seen Ebenezer look so grave.

"Why should this war bring trouble to Acadia? We're neutral. Can't things just go on as before?"

"There's a new governor, Charles Lawrence. He's not like the others, Mascarene or Hopson, who tried to understand the Acadians. He's a soldier and he wants to see Nova Scotia made secure for the British, not half-filled with French-speaking Acadians. He can't believe that they can be loyal to the king and yet unwilling to bear arms. They're in a trap, caught between the English and the French. Lawrence is a man of iron heart and I fear that he might deal with the Acadians more harshly than they can imagine."

"Please," Timothy begged. "The summer is so beautiful here. Let me stay. What can happen in a few months? I'm useful here and there's not much I can do in Boston to help."

"It worries me, Timothy, and your father will be disappointed, but very well. I'll be back at the end of the summer for you."

Relieved that his father was improving, Timothy put Ebenezer's sombre words out of his mind. He didn't want to think of such unpleasant matters in his green and blossoming valley.

He remembered them uneasily, however, the day the British soldiers came from Fort Edward to confiscate the Acadian sloops and schooners. Not even their canoes were spared.

Timothy and Martin stood in the churchyard with Uncle Pascal, watching silently as the last canoe vanished up the river, unsteadily paddled by its red-coated navigator.

"Why are they doing this?" Timothy raged. "Why do you let them? How will we fish?"

"The British suspect us of helping the French troops at Chignecto," Uncle Pascal said heavily. "How can we stop them, Boiteau? We are still King George's loyal subjects, even if Governor Lawrence does not believe it. Such things have happened before and we have survived."

One day, late in June, a party of New England troops landed unexpectedly near Minas. They belonged to a much larger force that had been recruited to drive the French from Fort Beauséjour on the Isthmus of Chignecto—which was almost eighty miles away. The people were told that the troops were on a grand fishing party as a reward for their courage at Beauséjour.

That night as Timothy and Martin were coming home from hunting, they saw two of the blue-coated soldiers knocking on the door of the house.

"Hey, boy," said one with a long narrow face dominated by a large bony nose. "Where is this famous Acadian hospitality we hear so much about?"

"Come in," Martin said politely, once Timothy had translated.

"Cider," demanded one of the Yankees in a loud, arrogant voice. "French brandy for me," ordered the other. "Nothing but the best from his Majesty's loyal Acadians." He laughed and put his dusty boots on Aunt Madeleine's well-scoured table.

Timothy was angered by this but reminded himself that soldiers were not known for their good manners. "I'm from New England too," he said. "Do you know my brother-in-law, Ebenezer Trumble? He's a merchant."

"A merchant?" Bony Nose winked at his companion, then bowed. "I'm pleased to meet such a fine Bostonian. Allow me to

introduce myself. I am King Louis of France and this is King George."

Timothy was infuriated by their mockery. But when Aunt Madeleine and Uncle Pascal returned from visiting friends the soldiers were polite and even complimented Aunt Madeleine on her rabbit stew.

Timothy and Martin had to sleep in the barn that night because the soldiers were given their bed. But Timothy couldn't sleep. The hay prickled and the memory of the soldiers' rudeness still rankled.

Quietly, in order not to disturb Martin, he got up and went out into the yard.

There was a light in the cabin window. "Aunt Madeleine must be awake," he thought. "Maybe we can have a cup of spruce tea to help us both sleep."

When he opened the door, he saw, not Aunt Madeleine raking the embers or talking to the dog or putting the kettle on the fire, he saw the Yankees ransacking the house.

Aunt Madeleine and Uncle Pascal sat together on a chest. The younger soldier held a musket to their heads.

"What are you doing?" Timothy cried.

"Searching the house for arms and ammunition, young'un," Bony Nose said cheerfully. "Can you read or are you unlettered like your relatives? Here's our orders." He shoved the parchment under Timothy's nose. "Now, boy, show us where they've hidden the rest of 'em."

"There's nothing to hide," Timothy said. "We only use guns for hunting food and to protect ourselves from wild beasts."

"That's as may be. What kind of New Englander are you anyhow, living here among these Frenchmen?"

"I'm ashamed to *be* a New Englander now!" Timothy shouted.

Bony Nose ignored him. "What's this?" He picked up a small porringer that Ebenezer had brought Aunt Madeleine and inspected it. "This is the work of a Boston silversmith, I'll be bound. What's it doing here? I'll just take it along for safekeeping."

By this time, Martin, sleepy-eyed, appeared in the doorway. Bony Nose glanced at him. "Over there in the corner with you." He shoved Martin on top of the chest with his parents.

"This is one of the good houses," he informed the family. "We are grateful for your kindness and your generous hospitality."

The soldiers collected a few more light valuables and departed with the dawn. No house in Minas was spared that night.

Shortly afterwards a proclamation went forth that all arms and ammunition still in the Acadians' possession were to be delivered up within ten days or the inhabitants would be treated as rebels and outlaws.

Helpless against the power of their British rulers, the Acadians obeyed.

"No ships, no guns. What are we to do?" Timothy asked Martin as they lay exhausted by the summer heat.

"Father says that the Deputies are going to ask the Governor in Halifax to give us back enough firearms to protect ourselves and the cattle against the bears that prowl in the woods," Martin said. "But it will be useless. This time, Boiteau, I do not think we will be left in peace."

Timothy remembered Ebenezer's sombre warning. "I wish those soldiers hadn't been from New England." He was almost crying. "I'm surprised you don't hate me. I wish they'd been from—from—oh blast!" He buried his face in the fresh grass.

"Hate you!" Martin said, surprised. "Why should I? Why should you be blamed for the evil deeds of others! You're my cousin and friend. Come, the Yankees may have taken away our guns and our boats but we can still go swimming."

In late July, Uncle Pascal left for Halifax with the Deputies from the other villages. They would continue in their loyalty to King George but would not bear arms against the French lest the Mi'kmaq unleash their anger against their families. The Indians and Acadians had long been friends, but the Mi'kmaq were also loyal allies of the French.

Governor Lawrence's response was to lock them up on Georges Island, as prisoners of war.

When word reached Minas that the Deputies were imprisoned and that Pascal Poirier was a captive, despair fell upon the village.

Timothy and Martin did their best to comfort Aunt Madeleine. Martin scarcely slept at all, he was so busy at his father's tasks. Timothy helped him and sang the jolliest sea shanties that he could remember. He also thought long and hard about Ebenezer's words. Perhaps it was time to go back to Boston and take his aunt and cousin with him. Uncle Pascal could follow when he was released. He couldn't be kept a prisoner forever.

Timothy bounded into the house where Aunt Madeleine was, as usual, doing three things at once: weeping, praying and making a heavy shirt to send to Uncle Pascal.

"We can't stay here much longer," he said. "When Ebenezer returns, you must come with us to Boston."

His aunt looked at him and sighed. "I could never live away from here," she declared. "This is my home."

"But the soldiers tell us every day that you will have to leave anyhow," Timothy insisted. "Martin, make her listen. You're all sitting here waiting for what?"

"It's been like this for forty years," Martin reminded him. "If it were just me, I'd escape to the woods and go north. But we Acadians have decided that it shall be one and all. Each person will share in our people's fate. If any one of us is removed, not one will remain. Whatever trials await us, we choose not to be divided."

"Dear Timothy," Aunt Madeleine said, her voice full of concern. "You must return to your father as soon as Ebenezer comes. We will think of you often."

Timothy felt an overwhelming despair and confusion.

Several weeks passed and still the Deputies did not come home. There were no parties in the small houses now, nor blueberry-picking expeditions, nor services in the church. All the priests of Acadia had been imprisoned in Halifax along with the Deputies. Small groups of frightened people clustered in the pathway to exchange news, scattering at the approach of the grim-faced soldiers from the makeshift camp at the parish church in nearby Grand-Pré.

Timothy had no wish to speak to his fellow New Englanders now, but he listened to their conversations as they strolled along, helping themselves to the ripening fruit and vegetables in the gardens.

"You *must* believe that you're to be sent away," he told Aunt Madeleine. "You will be put on ships to sail who knows where. The English are not afraid of an uprising because they have taken away all your guns. The soldiers even joke about it and call it the Acadian Toothdrawing. They want lists of family members so that they won't be separated."

Aunt Madeleine refused to believe it. "They've been threatening this for years," she said. "Let the British say what they please, they're only trying to frighten us into submission. Soon they'll release my Pascal and life will go on as before."

But later that day Timothy found her in the orchard burying her most precious treasures wrapped in birchbark.

It was September 5. The boys and men of the district had been ordered to assemble at the church in Grand-Pré. Timothy, Martin, Aunt Madeleine and the other women and children of the village followed them—they would watch the proceedings from outside the palisade surrounding the church.

Talking noisily among themselves, the more than four hundred boys and men, Martin's brothers among them, entered the church. There, in the centre, a table was set up and several officers were standing by.

"Silence!" shouted Colonel Winslow, the man in charge. Pointing to Jacques Landry and a few others who stood in the front row, the colonel ordered them to record the name of every Acadian there.

At three o'clock, after the last name had been entered and the books were signed, Colonel Winslow raised a handkerchief and gestured to his interpreters that he was ready to read the order. The Acadian inhabitants, it said—men women and children all—were to be deported. They forfeited to the Crown their land, houses and livestock, and could take with them from the province only money and the household goods that the ships could carry.

The boys and men were shocked into silence, their faces filled with disbelief.

"These instructions are disagreeable to me," Colonel Winslow said, "but I must obey such orders as I receive them. You are now prisoners of war. You will be confined and must await the will of the government." With this Winslow and his men departed, locking the doors of the church behind them.

"The will of God be done," Jacques Landry sighed. "So be it," chorused his brothers and, pulling on their hats, they accepted their fate.

The dreadful silence within was not echoed without. From the moment the men had passed beyond the palisade, the women and children had stood rooted to the ground, watching and waiting. They could hear no sounds of violence from within the palisades, but they knew something was terribly wrong. They shuddered when they saw that the garrison was under arms. When the gates were barred and sentinels took up their positions, a sudden scream arose. This mournful cry passed from village to village throughout the whole district of Minas. Nothing had been said, but the people knew that their fathers and brothers were now prisoners, like the elders crowded together on Georges Island.

Timothy and Martin half-led, half-carried the weeping Aunt Madeleine to the house of a cousin to take shelter for the night. They were exhausted, more from grief than travel, and sat down to rest along the way. As the sun went down that dreadful day, a brilliant flood of light spread over the sky. The clouds looked like islands floating on a calm sea of blue and gold. They formed images of palaces, gardens, terraces and archways.

"It is a better place up there." Aunt Madeleine wiped her eyes and smiled through the hot tears. "It is the pure home of the angels. This is a message to the afflicted Acadians that we will dwell in happiness together once more when our trials are over. Come, my children, we will go to Mireille's house now."

But as the darkness settled in, Aunt Madeleine grew anxious again. She was not alone—no one could sleep. Pine torches blazed in every direction. Friend met friend and asked for word of the prisoners. Children wandered about alone, crying and unheeded. The cattle, unmilked, lowed their distress. Dogs, abandoned beside unlit fireplaces, howled dismally. It was a bitter night in Acadia.

For two days the people mourned. Then, early on the third morning, the gates of the camp swung open and seven of the older prisoners came out. Immediately they were surrounded by friends and families and greeted with joyful cries and anxious questions.

"What is to happen to us?"

"Are we to suffer and die together or are we to be driven to distraction by tortures without a name?"

"We do not know where we are to be sent," said one of the prisoners. "But all our lands and cattle and crops are forfeit. We can take our money with us and some pieces of furniture if they are not too heavy. That is all they have told us."

"Where are my sons?" Aunt Madeleine asked. "Where are René, Daniel and Mathieu?" She trembled as she spoke and leaned heavily on Timothy's arm.

"We have been sent to comfort you," said the oldest prisoner. "But our visit must be short. We will be punished if we stay too long. Be of good cheer, for each morning and evening, some of you can visit us in the church for an hour."

This promise brought relief to the women and children and they began to sing:

> *Carry the cross*
> *When we serve it from choice*
> *Though it is very bitter and very hard—*
> *In spite of man and nature,*
> *Carry the cross—*

Although she was reluctant to leave Grand-Pré with her sons imprisoned there, Aunt Madeleine was persuaded by Martin and Timothy to return home. They had been told that the transports would soon arrive to take them away.

A few German-speaking settlers from Lunenberg came to gather the crops and some Yankee troops drove away the cattle, but Martin had time to hide the favourite cow in a thick stand of bush, so they had milk and the few vegetables not stripped from the garden.

It was October and still the transports did not come.

"Soon," Timothy thought, "Ebenezer will be here. Then we will all be safe." He packed his few belongings in order to be ready to leave at once.

The mists were swirling in from the bay on the morning that William brought a message. Timothy met him at the door as he was on his way in with a few sticks of wood for the fire.

"We're anchored in the bay by the new dyke," William said. "You're to come at once." He plunged back into the mist like a sturdy phantom.

"He's here!" Timothy found his aunt and cousin sitting gazing into the tiny fire in the giant fireplace where once huge logs had burned. "We'll soon be safe. Come quickly."

Martin looked at him calmly, but said nothing. Aunt Madeleine embraced him. "Goodbye, dear Timothy. We will stay."

Timothy could not believe it. "You *must* come. No one knows what will become of us here."

Martin shook his head.

"But we'd be happy together," Timothy pleaded. "We'd forget all this." He was frightened by what he saw around him and he wanted to flee to safety. But he found it almost impossible to move. How could he leave his Acadian family to an uncertain fate! Finally, Timothy hoisted his pack on his shoulder and, followed by the faithful Nip, walked along the overgrown pathway. Through the mists he went, avoiding the pathetic heaps of belongings that had been piled outside by the distraught women. The scarlet and gold leaves of fall, rusted and mildewed by the rain, lay in dank heaps.

He trudged on past the Mass House. The lawn was overgrown and no flowers bloomed now on the tall white crosses. Only their blackened skeletons remained. He passed a drunken soldier, who looked at him curiously but said nothing. It took a long time to reach the little hidden bay where *The Reliant* was anchored. He looked around in the fog. The figure of Ebenezer detached itself from a concealing tree.

"Good lad. What kept you?"

"Many things." Timothy sighed and dropped his pack to the ground. "Give my love to Father and Priscilla," he said unsteadily.

"What are you talking about?" Ebenezer bent down to pick up the pack. Nip laid back her ears and growled. Timothy reached out to calm her.

"I'm staying here," he whispered. "I can't go back to Boston. Tell Father and he'll understand." He told Ebenezer about all that had happened.

Ebenezer looked at him in silence for a moment. "Well, lad," he said slowly, "you face a grim future, but I'm not going to try to dissuade you. You're old enough to make up your own mind. God go with you and grant that we meet again in happier times." He embraced the boy, smiled sadly and was gone.

Timothy started back towards home. On the way he found a wild plum tree.

"This will please Aunt Madeleine." He pulled the frost-bitten plums from the tree. Wizened and sour though they might be, they would be a welcome treat in these hungry times.

The fog was lifting and masses of clouds were battling each other for mastery of the sky. Long streaks of gleaming light were flung from the warring cloud battalions. Their colour changed from snowy white to icy green.

"Such strange colours," Timothy thought. These reflections suddenly gave place to others—blood red, bright orange— against the jet black of the forest.

No, these were not strange reflections in the sky. As Timothy came over the crest of the hill, he saw columns of black smoke rising from the village. Minas was ablaze. There were four ships out in the bay.

"The transports have come!" he cried aloud. Timothy began to run. He ran as he had never run before, but it seemed to take forever.

He stopped, gasping for breath, with a stitch in his side, at the outskirts of the village. Smoke filled the air. There were soldiers everywhere. He could hardly move without bumping into someone or something: carts of furniture, boys staggering under the weight of trunks with dogs barking at their heels.

Some houses were in ashes, others were in flames, burning like torches. Worst of all was the noise. The old women who used to sit gossiping by the well were making a horrible wailing sound. They beat the walls with their hands and tore at their black shawls and dresses.

Timothy ran to his house and went inside but there was no one there. On his way out he met two soldiers. They had flaring torches and were about to set fire to the building.

"Stop, wait. Don't burn this house," he cried. They looked up quickly when they heard the English words but relaxed when they saw it was only a young Acadian.

"We got our orders, lad, and even if we don't like 'em, we got to do it all the same. Some of the Acadians have slipped away to the woods. We can't have 'em sneaking back and setting up here again."

Nearby a burning house collapsed and sent thousands of sparks flying. Several landed on Nip, who yelped in pain.

Timothy ran towards the wharf, to find Aunt Madeleine and Martin. But it was even more confusing there. The beach was piled with boxes, baskets and bundles. Crowds of weeping women and children were being pushed towards the longboats by soldiers.

Timothy hurried from group to group, Nip barking at his heels. "Have you seen Aunt Madeleine! Has anyone seen Martin?"

He could hear no answer except the crackling of flames and the tragic cries of women and children.

"Here, what are you doing standing about?" The sharp point of a musket poked his back. "Into the longboat with you." Timothy turned around and saw a soldier pushing him towards the water. Just then he saw Aunt Madeleine. She was struggling to help Martin lift a box of their belongings into a longboat. Timothy broke away and ran to them.

"Wait for me," he cried. "Aunt Madeleine, Martin, wait for me!" They stared bleakly as if they didn't recognize him. Aunt Madeleine's face was pale, Martin's was smeared with soot and blood from a gash in his forehead.

Nip's frantic barks broke their trance.

"Timothy," Aunt Madeleine faltered. "I hoped you were safely off with Ebenezer." She sat down suddenly on the box and began to weep. The damp mists swirled in off the bay and mingled with the smoke.

"I decided to stay," he said, comforting her. "Don't cry, Aunt Madeleine. We'll be together."

"Idiot," said Martin, coughing from the acrid smoke. "Now you'll be a homeless wanderer, too." But he smiled and added, "God bless you anyway."

Timothy looked steadily at his family. "One and all," he said. They helped Aunt Madeleine into the longboat and heaved the box in after her.

"Hurry up there, you!" shouted a soldier. Nip bared her teeth and growled. "All right, all right, good girl." The soldier retreated a few paces. "The dog can't go," he snarled.

Nip stood whining on the shore. Timothy leaned down to stroke her soft head. "You always hated water," he told her gently. "You'll be better off here. Home, Nip!" he shouted and she ran off into the fog and smoke. Timothy and Martin climbed aboard.

In the growing darkness they were all herded into the transports. In the end, most of their goods were abandoned on the shore. They were crowded to near suffocation, packed together like cattle on the slippery decks. They sat, shivering in the cold, silently watching the bright orange flames up and down the coast.

"We need a song, Timothy," Martin said. "It will comfort everybody."

Quietly at first, Timothy began to sing the song that had swept through the villages during the time of their trials. "Gather and join us, or give us a grave." He sang again. "We will return to the land of our ancestors, our beloved land. We Acadians will return."

Proud and clear his voice rang over the water, as darkness descended on that last night in Acadia.

THE SMALL DOG lay panting in the shade of a drooping willow. The hollow shell of the ruined house she guarded was hidden by a healing web of wild roses. Only the outline of the bench by the deserted well could be seen through the mass of green leaves and riotous blossoms.

The dog pricked her ears at an unaccustomed sound in the silence, which was usually broken only by the hum of a wild bee or the cry of an animal. With short urgent barks she ran down the hill to see who was invading her kingdom.

In the bay was an old boat with a ragged sail. Half-savage after three years alone, the small dog hid behind a bush and watched, growling softly.

The boat drifted closer. The dog ran to the shore, jumped into the water and paddled out. She scratched impatiently on the side of the boat until Timothy hauled her in. She shook herself, spraying him with water, then began to lick their faces.

"Nip!" Timothy hugged the small wet dog.

They had spent many years in Maryland as indentured servants after the deportation, then months working their way up the Atlantic coast in their homemade boat, creeping ashore by night to sleep and to find food. But Timothy, Martin and Aunt Madeleine together with hundreds of other exiled Acadians, like the wild geese they knew so well, had returned to their northern home.

Afterword

A CADIAN LIFE IN the first half of the eighteenth century was much as Timothy saw it, a rich complex existence in a turbulent age. In the 1750s, the Acadians were the largest group of people in Atlantic Canada. The English ruled over them and the French were on the boundaries of their lands. The Indian people moved freely throughout the whole area. Such a mixture made the Acadian community volatile even in times of peace; but in times of war between the English and the French, Acadian life was dangerous indeed.

For nearly a century and a half, as the French and English struggled for mastery in North America, the Acadians managed to develop and preserve an independence from both super-powers. The Acadians knew that their lands formed a frontier between the two great empires, and like any other border people, they wanted to avoid taking sides. Although most of their ancestors came from village backgrounds in France, some had come from Scotland, Ireland, and the ports of England. By the 1630s there were English-speaking people in Acadia. This meant that while the language and culture of the Acadians developed from French roots, the English language was known in the villages. Acadians traded as often with the English as with the French.

So what Timothy found in the 1750s was a strongly knit, independent community that was used to being under pressure from stronger powers. Those powers were now demanding total allegiance—which the Acadians were unwilling to give. The savagery of imperial war between England and France destroyed the first Acadian community, but soon after their deportation, the Acadians began to return. By 1764 they were once more rebuilding a life in the Maritimes and creating communities that were as distinct, as unique, and as vivid as had been those that were destroyed in 1755.

— *Naomi E.S. Griffiths*